What a Hullabaloo!

by
Phillip Whittington

Cover illustration by Maggie Shaffer

authorHOUSE®

AuthorHouse™ UK Ltd.
500 Avebury Boulevard
Central Milton Keynes, MK9 2BE
www.authorhouse.co.uk
Phone: 08001974150

© 2009 Phillip Whittington. All rights reserved.

No part of this book may be reproduced, stored in a retrieval system, or transmitted by any means without the written permission of the author.

First published by AuthorHouse 8/24/2009

ISBN: 978-1-4389-9219-8 (sc)

This book is printed on acid-free paper.

To

Emma for coping.
Jonathan Masters, who sadly passed away on the 7th April 2002, whose inspirations are very much alive in the verses of this book.
Michael Masters, for those early days.
Maggie Shaffer for doing such an excellent job with the cover illustration.
The SCPTI gang for believing.
Veronica Murray for helping me to believe.
Chris Pittordou and Margaret McSauly Walker for memories, and verses yet to be written!
Hilly, Birchy and the rest of the gang.
Parents and brother.

Contents

Nipper in Slipper 1
Wasp in Beard 7
Four Paws of Claws 15
The Green Head of Man 23
Foot in Pond 30
Sandwich in Sock 36
Apple on Foot 41

Nipper in Slipper

It was Friday night teatime on sleepover day
When me and the gang got the call to stop play
So we headed inside to where parent was shouting
To kitchen where dog looked for bowl to put snout in

We sat round the table all elbows and spoons
And gulped when we saw what came into the room
Five plates of liver with onions on side
And cabbage and parsnips along for the ride

Now this wasn't Friday night sleepover stuff
And seeing it we knew it would not be enough
So we planned that at midnight when parents were sleeping
The gang would go creeping to kitchen for sweet things

The parents threw wobblers when good food was wasted
So plates must be emptied before they were tasted
So under the table old four paws was slurping
And chewing and chomping and drooling and burping

When liver filled dog was asleep under table
And plates were as clean as a Trojan horse stable
We slipped off to sofa to watch the cartoons
And yawned each time parents came into the room

We knew that we had to make parents believe that
The gang was as tired as a melon filled fruit bat
And when parents sent us to bed base for sleep
They'd go themselves early and leave us to creep

And so there we waited, as quiet as mice
Except for the odd noise that didn't smell nice
And listened while parents put false teeth in cups
With labels on sides so they didn't mix them up

Now I know that your thinking you want us to swap them
But last time we did that caused parent to drop them
And dog that was passing at time did a pounce
And charged off to lounge making crunching type sounds

Two hundred pounds was the bill for the biters
And vet had to check dog was not chewed inside her
So teeth were quite safe on the sink side this evening
And ready for breakfast the tusks would be gleaming

The time went so slowly for weary gang waiting
But thoughts of the sweet stuff meant none were complaining
And when we heard light switch of parent go click
Five mouths of gang stuck out tongue to lick lip

We crept from the bedroom one foot at a time
Five pairs of legs with ten feet in a line
And crept past the snore doors where parents were sleeping
Not noticing four paws had joined the feet creeping

The dog she had heard us and hot on our heels
She licked lips and wagged tail amidst doggy squeals
And this wasn't good for the noise would wake sleepers
So dog's tail was socked up and hidden were squeakers

Just then we heard rattling and whirring and clanging
The hamster had woken and red wheel was banging
So one lad was sent back to room to put spanner in
The works of the wheel that the hamster ran round in

But as he put hand in to halt the contraption
The hamster with long tooth found soft spot to latch on
And as he whipped hand out through hamster proof door
The nipper came with it and dropped to the floor

Now hamsters have eyes that were made for the dark
And big dog with socked tail had mouth made to bark
So all sorts of madness and hullabaloo
Erupted when dog saw small rat in the room

The lad quick grabbed dog's snout and wrestled it to floor
Whilst wild whippet hamster quick ran for the door
And as we were too far away to quick snatch him
He waddled through small gap in snore door on landing

The parents were sleeping and snoring and grunting
With bed socks on big feet and not hamster hunting
So safer it was in that room full of noise
Than out on the landing with barefooted boys

So we shut the door quietly and left him to trundle
Through slippers and spy books and rolled up wool bundles
Then calmed down the big dog by waggling a finger
Through bars of the beast's cage so she'd think he's in there

Then once again ten feet sneaked off down the hallway
With small torch from dads bike to light up the doorway
We also had satchel from school to put grub in
To take chop to room for some mad midnight munching

The torch lit up lovely the traps on the landing
The hat racks and boot stands that parents found handy
And those at the front of the long line of short legs
Had no trouble missing the things that could bump heads

But the lad at the back who was last in the line
Was furthest from light and did not see with eye
The shelf that stood low on the wall with a phone on
Which he bashed while passing his small elbow bone on

Now a funny bone's not funny if you give it a clatter
In fact you could best say it's no laughing matter
And such was the case for the lad who'd bashed elbow
And the funny thing was it was funny for us though

He stood there in torchlight with whole hand in mouth
To block out the shout that now tried to get out
While we held our stomachs and noses to keep in
A noise that was equal to banged elbow bone din

Then finally we reached it, the treasure filled food room
Where parents whilst cooking sung songs in a strange tune
And small boys were told off for breaking an ant farm
And dog opened fridge door with furry-clawed dog arm

We knew that on high shelf the best stuff was hidden
Where short arms couldn't reach 'em and dogs couldn't sniff 'em
So somehow we had to add length to a lad
So lad could reach higher and hand could then grab

For that shelf had sweets we could only have one of
And fizzy things that parents wouldn't let us take top off
And next to these treats was the bestest of all
The tin we were told contained nothing at all!!

So long lad was chosen to climb up to grab it
On three-legged stool with a bad wobble habit
And knowing that safety came first with the gang
The long lad felt safe doing wobbly stool plan

Now it happened that long lad was scared stiff of spiders
And a high place was good place for hairy-legged hiders
And as he reached high up to grab tin with hand
He grabbed something different than what he had planned

There in his hand was a flat backed black wriggler
With eyes big as buttons and legs thick as fingers
And as he tried quickly to shake beast from palm
The eight-legged fly biter quick shot up his arm

Now a spider in T-shirt was not what was needed
Whilst wobbling on small stool an inch from the ceiling
And lesson in gravity that's quick learnt when high up
Is boys aren't like cats that can fall down and stand up

He came down as quick as a chimp that had stepped on
A branch with banana skin someone had left on
And formed a gang tangle of small boys that wriggled
Like a pond full of tadpoles with an eel in the middle

Now four paws went bonkers when gang was there tied up
And howling she jumped high on five-boy gang pile up
And chomped with a sharp tooth the first foot she found
Which brought forth a half muffled shout from the mound

Now a parent that's woken by barking and bumping
Is not in the best mood when half asleep clumping
And things just got worse when he popped on a slipper
To find soft place taken by furry toothed nipper

Now the nipper wasn't happy being squashed by a foot
And so on the big digit of foot it did put
A nice curvy nut-breaking, bar-chewing tooth
That made foot go spring-like and parent hit roof

Whilst stood in the kitchen we heard parents screaming
For the other had woken to madness from dreaming
And knowing that seconds we had just to get to
The safety of bed base we'd built in the bedroom

So off we went quickly with hands full of sweet things
As fizzy pop fizzed up in fizzy pop fizz tins
And got back to bedroom as snore door was creaking
And hid before head of the parent came peeking

We slipped beneath blankets and all made a snore noise
So parents wouldn't think they'd been woken by small boys
And as the door opened I sneaked a quick look
At parent with big hair and slipper-less foot

He gazed for a moment at gang that was sleeping
At nine eyes closed tightly all facing the ceiling
Then looked back behind him at four pawed black sniffer
Howling at hamster head poking from slipper

So nipper was captured and finally caged up
By tiptoeing parent who tried not to wake us
And dog was then locked up in cold porch 'til morning
For barking and howling and midnight performing

When wandering parents at last were back sleeping
And no dogs were barking or hamster heads peeping
We sat there in bed den all quietly munching
And sucking crisps slowly to silence the crunching

Now we should have remembered, we should have but didn't
That pop that is shook up is quite fond of fizzing
So as can was opened and from it came fizz
The light switch of parent we heard again click!!

Wasp in Beard

Silently I crept from kitchen to lounge
With jammy buttered slice in my jammy buttered hand
Plates were not needed when parents were asleep
But sound of a mess, could make parent creep
So aware-full and careful I sneaked like a sneaker
Past trip rugs and floorboards loud fitted with squeakers

When reaching the lounge jammy slice was then placed on
The arm of the sofa the dog had its nest on
And as I sat chomping with black dog foot pawing
I heard secret bird noise of gang outside calling

So I placed a big cushion on new stain on sofa
And hoped that the sofa police didn't flip it over
And thought I'd be good boy and keep the house nice
So I called dog to kitchen to lick jam off knife

The gang was there ready and waiting at gate
On bikes of all colours and all kinds of states
Some had high handles with gear stick in middle
And one had a flat tyre and one had no saddle

If brakes didn't work we'd just stop with our feet
But too fast for feet meant the grazing of knees
But that didn't stop us at all we were tough
And when teachers couldn't hear we said all kinds of stuff

Now strong lad in gang was as hard as old flint
And in pocket to prove toughness kept an Extra Strong Mint
And if girls, gangs or parents dared challenge our plans
The strong mint of toughness would come out in hand
And if that didn't stop 'em the mint would be placed
On tongue and he'd suck it and not change his face

So, ready we were on this parent-free morning
As cool autumn air mixed with bike oil and yawning
We saddled up swiftly and set off to find
The conkers for this time was conkering time

Before we set peddling with foot to the place
We visited sweet shop where toothaches were made
And stocked up with sherbets, Cherry Lips and bubbly
And something that quick fizzed and gassed you up lovely
We also bought Black Jacks, Fruit Salads and gums
And set off for conker with Black Jack type tongues

The journey to tree field was far and was filled with
The short cuts we knew well and hills that would seem big
To lad with no bike seat who'd stand going down
With no brakes on bike wheels and big type of frown

We passed the old army base covered in vines
That closed because zombies were made there in wartime
At least that's what parents at campsite had told us
Whilst we listened for the bones of those skeleton soldiers

We peddled a little faster, with no signs of scaredness
Not thinking of green skulls all shiny and hairless
And sang as we past it with voices so loud
That nothing could be heard making clinking bone sounds

At last we had reached it the turn off to gate
And for saddle-less rider we pulled up to wait
For whilst thinking of zombies the lad had got flustered
And steered into deep ditch with big nettle clusters

We crept from the roadside to gate of the farmer
Who'd locked it with big lock to make entrance harder
But this wouldn't stop us as training we'd had in
The art of gate climbing and high tree branch grabbing

So over we went with our bikes on our shoulders
The conker gang bike-carrying gate-climbing soldiers
And searched for the treasured brown nuts that would make us
The kings of the playground and lords of the school bus

We avoided the wheat fields and scarecrow type watchers
That farmer had grown there to secretly watch us
And headed for cow field which had an old bath
And brown cow crop circles all over the grass

The last time we'd seen him he'd chased us with stick
But farmers aren't shaped the shape to be quick
And as mud flew around him from big flapping feet
He held up his trousers with hand that was free

We didn't mean to bug him but something went wrong
When the old gate we'd swung on was not quite as strong
As the weight of a gang that held tight as it bowed
'Til gate came off hinges and cows went up road

He said that he'd catch us and with big boot would boot us
And then he'd get big gun from farmhouse to shoot us
So gang didn't wait there to let the man catch up
We scarpered like Mexican mice from a cat shop

We walked across cow fields aware of the bull
That eyed us with eye whilst enjoying a chew
And I thought that with big horn that bull might try stab me
For I'd never seen a bull on a hill that was happy

Now people who fight bulls don't fight them with bikes
And being chased by a bull pushing my bike I wouldn't like
So quickly we passed with no red things bright showing
Apart from our sweaty heads puffing and blowing

We reached the high hilltop and spied down below
For signs of mad farmer stood watching things grow
And seeing the coast clear we charged down the slope
The bike brigade charged down to conkers below

We stood there as challengers with brave hero faces
With bamboo sticks, bubblegum and someone's dad's braces
We also had with us the dream to find big one
Some large purple pants and a strong string to rig them

Now catapults were good things for King Arthur's round Knights
Who quick knocked down high walls of castles in big fights
But never could gang get enough twang to sling up
A stick or a stone to hard hit conker high up

So braces were thrown up in tree where they stayed
With red pair from last year and boomerang we'd made
That never quite came back with conker well stuck to
The edges we'd plastered with strong parent wood glue

The bamboo was strong though with many a long shoot
And we knew that one day that we'd find plan to suit
Such a long thing that bended from country with swords
Where people used hard heads and hands to break boards

We taped up the bamboo and bubble gummed each length
'Til bamboo was longer than snake could be stretched
And laid it on floor amid brown cow crop circles
And added to top with strong string the pants purple

We knew that this tower of wood would reach high up
And pants would catch conker in leg that was tied up
And bamboo would bend and not break at the seams
For yesterday it held up a parents french beans

We'd planned up this plan because two things we'd found
The first was that conkers didn't always hit ground
And sometimes they bounced not and came to a stop
In piles of what cows left behind with a plop

Secondly the conker drops hard from up high
And it's best if you're under to not look with eye
For one of the gang who had looked gained a bump
That turned to a conker shaped conker coloured lump

But before we caught conker we first had to check
Just who could jump over the wide muddy beck
As last year this challenge had beat all but one
And everyone but one had a mud plastered bum

But this didn't stop me as I flew from the ground
And got a full halfway over before fully coming down
And once again backside met mud with a splat
And shoe flew from foot into crop circle pat

So re-shoed and muddied we headed to the tree
With squelches in school shoes and grazes on knees
And I had a lovely big bruise on my ankle
And cow muck in shoelaces double knot tied tangle

The lad with the strong arm then climbed onto branch
To wallop the conkers with stick into pants
And this was a good plan and no plan was better
And nothing would go wrong with this plan, not ever!

So wallop them he did with a massive big blow
And we saw them miss pants as we watched from below
So we ducked and we dived as the tree bullets fell
To bruise us and bash us and prickle us as well

We probably should have noticed when buzzing occurred
That a nest full of small things with stings was disturbed
And out from a hole that had just gained a conker
Came a yellow striped gang going totally bonkers

For strong lad at this time on branch up in tree
Probably wasn't the best place to be
And as we danced wildly our wasp dance below
He held stomach laughing enjoying the show

But wasps are not stupid and the striped little stingers
Quick buzzed up tall tree and stung him on finger
Which would have been ok and not caused much fuss
If it hadn't been on hand that was holding him up

So down he came swiftly with conkers and all
And a big gang of wasps and a bike broke his fall
But luckily for him when with cow muck was covered
He found that the clean wasps were not cow muck lovers

Now all this performance and hullabaloo
Had caught the attention of a sheep dog or two
That licked us and sniffed us and got a tum scratching
'Til farmers head popped up with growling teeth gnashing

Now farmers get madder than a parent who's found
That a ball's broke his greenhouse and no-one's around
And fast he came screaming in brown suit and boots
With a face red as apples and big gun that shoots

Now the farmer's loud shouting on other side of fence
Attracted the attention of our little yellow friends
Who hearing the commotion popped over to say
Hello to the farmer as we ran to gate

Over it we were in the blink of an eye
With conkers and wasp stings, carrying our bikes
And not looking back because loud sounds were heard
From barking mad farmer with big wasp in beard

Laughing we peddled because he'd not caught us
But farmer knew short cuts that we'd never thought of
And cunning was farmer and slipperier than eel
As he slipped through a small hole in hedge of the field

But farmer wasn't lucky unless it was fate
For he'd jumped out in front of my mate with no brakes
And it happened that the handlebars of my mates bike
Smacked poor old farmer in a place he didn't like

Now lad who had snagged him he had to quick run
Before farmer could grab him to put boot on bum
So he jumped on the back of my bike and clung tight
As I peddled like a wing flapping moth to a light

We got home much quicker than a car full of rockets
And on kitchen table we emptied our pockets
Of cow muck and conkers and dead wasp gone stiff
Which quickly we placed on mate's dad's pie in fridge

We thought we'd surprise then our friend's biggest sister
By placing the prickly part of conker in slipper
To get her back good-style for the prank in canteen
At school when she'd filled up my pocket with beans

This could have been payback for when we mixed ink with
The silky smooth shampoo she'd left by the sink
Far too much fuss because blond hair went blue
And she got a free haircut and two days off school

We then started wrestling for spare conker left
Which was big as a beetroot and better than the rest
But the tussle soon ended when parent pushed door
And bumped head of lad caught in headlock on floor

Now parent wasn't happy one bit about finding
That five-conker ninjas in kitchen were fighting
And nor was she happy about cow muck on side
Or the teeth marks in crust of mate's dad's wasp topped pie

So grumbling and groaning she showed us the door
Whilst passing a mop to my mate to mop floor
Then quickly we grabbed bikes to get space between us
Before she thought different and made us help clean up

Other tales will tell of what happened in playground
With conkers from this one and sister who's foot found
A spiky green shell thing attached to her toe
And where her dad's braces went, he'll never ever know!!

Four Paws of Claws

The gang were all packed up and walking down short street
In trousers that stopped at the top of a short knee
And entered the scout hut where big crowd was waiting
With cheeks red as rhubarb and nearly all shaking

The scout hut was colder than bare foot in winter
And smelt like the whole thing was made from a slipper
And as we walked over the boss one was counting
The tent bags and tent poles and pegs for tent grounding

Now this one had big beard and no hair on head top
And voice that was deeper than horn to make boat stop
And legs that you'd find joining feet to a pigeon
With high socks that ballcock-shaped knee couldn't fit in

The gang knew they'd have to be careful with this one
For spy in the Air Force he'd done before this job
And told us he knew every trick, joke or caper
That small lad could think up or work out on paper

So there we stood waiting for boss one and sidekick
To check every tent bag and bent peg inside it
For broke bits and live things that may have quick crept in
To make a nice nest out of things that we slept in

The sidekick had badges for hard type knot tying
And building of big fires and paper plane flying
And always did quick nod when boss one was talking
And counted our footsteps when marching-type walking

So needless to say that the gang wasn't happy
That tall nodding badge scout was joining us camping
And as he was driver of first bus in line
We got on the back one avoiding his eye

The driver of this one was grim and he told us
That back seat was not place for fooling on scout bus
And whilst he was sorting out straightness of hat
A big type of punch up broke out at the back

The strong lad had charged up and laid himself flat on
The whole row of back seats so none could be sat on
And lads close behind him with same kind of thoughts
Grabbed him and so began big type of war

Now twelve of us wrestling and shouting on back seat
Was noticed by driver in hat with a high peak
And loud is the voice of a hat wearer's anger
And more so when hat's sat on head of bus handler

We first saw the beard get on bus before full face
A thing that could pass line and win cup in fast race
And heaped up we waited for loud type of natter
Like time we'd placed gooseberry in granddad's grape platter

I should say at this point that silence was not quite
As golden as song said or lasting for long time
And gang knew that trapped voice would soon find its way
Through tight-tangled face-hair with loud things to say

And so it was said loud and not in a whisper
That trip would go well now without funny business
And as driver drove off he spoke of the days
When thin stick on backside taught kids to behave

The scout bus was stopped after just a few miles though
When one lad on back seat pressed bum flat on window
And car sat behind us with parent-aged bloke in
Got more than expected when Sunday type driving

So there we were standing by roadside in truck stop
Whilst driver told full tale of backside to scout boss
But stuck was the old one for picking out culprit
For cheeky grin shown him had no eyes or nose bit

The boss man with big beard I think then believed us
For no-one on scout bus at all had seen bum press
And strong lad had quick said that man had made error
And caught site of own face in window screen mirror

Now this didn't help much and after the shouting
We got back on scout bus and on with the outing
And silent was long trip with noise banned on bus
And beard sat in middle part of back seat with us

The campsite was small field with tents and big tree on
With tap on a low pipe the height to bang knee on
And up at the high end a big forest whispered
With scary type voices through leafy green fingers

Now even in daylight the forest had dark bits
And right behind our tent was darkest by far bit
And watched it we did as we tightened our lines
For shadows with heads full of big shiny eyes

The bloke that was tented in big tent beside us
Said things from the dark bits would not creep and bite us
For daylight was too light for such things to creep
And nighttime was best time for bad things to feed

He said that the last time he'd stayed there he'd heard that
A man who was tented on same spot that we had
Was startled on dark night by some kind of roaring
And woke up loud screaming with leg gone in morning

Now this bloke was big bloke with nose bashed from boxing
And birds-nest type eyebrows that eyes could get lost in
And as he told story, a gold tooth was shining
From mouth that had no teeth before or behind it

Whilst gang was stood listening to stories of lost limbs
And whistling of words passing lonely gold peg thing
We heard a shout slip through the beard of the leader
And went to grab long food from camp fire type feeder

The fire that he'd built was on big flat type stone thing
With something quite sink-like in hot bit with smoke in
And sidekick with big badge for 'Best Cook of Food'
Was handing out black things too hard for a tooth

The strong lad had said that he'd rather eat small things
That wriggled in old logs in forest with eyes in
And badged one who'd heard him whilst topping up plate
Sat back as sun set and told us a tale

He told us of wild woods and bare hand bear battling
And punch up with large skunk and snake that was rattling
And capture of strange thing with big hairy foot
That ran off with camera and photo he'd took

Now this bloke had done things that films only told of
And showed us his shark bites and holes made by soldiers
But gang thought it quite strange that shark bites and rockets
Had only left small marks on kneecap joint sockets

The badged one was too tall and wrong shape for tenting
And sleep bag was too short without a leg bending
And often in morning through tent flap was peeping
The foot that was famous for hungry shark feeding

The strong lad had woken on such a foot morning
And shook us and told us of plan he'd been forming
And thinking it good one we'd slipped out of beds
With sagging low middles and rusty type legs

We needed some bread so the small lad was chosen
To sneak under side flap of food tent and grab some
And as he went creeping we watched the sun rising
And thought how the badged one was ripe for surprising

The small lad was best lad for small place type creeping
And came back with shirt stuffed and loaf of bread peeping
And this plan was great plan and gang thought it better
Than bread plan that went wrong for Hansel and Gretel

We knew that the small pond would not have a shark in
And big woods were bear-less with no stinking skunks in
But strong lad had found well a new kind of beast
The kind we could quick temp to lovely foot feast

Silent and barefoot we stepped over tent pegs
And crept across wet grass whilst watching for worm heads
And headed for small group with triangle type toes
That looked like half circles in bright feather clothes

The ducks were all stood there in some kind of bird gang
Just waiting for tent things to wake up and feed 'em
And as we approached them with bread and bare feet
They wished they had duck tongues to lick end of beak

A good thing for us was that ducks were not far from
The place where a foot was with large piece of bread on
And trail that we'd laid there to join foot to beak
Was made from bread edges that ducks loved to eat

Now ducks that have waited since tea time for thrown bits
And slept with heads backwards well tucked up in wing tips
Are hungry like spaceman who'd just found on moon
He'd left his egg sandwich back home in his room

We had to move quick though for ducks that we'd woke up
Were fast on to short trail of bread that we'd broke up
And just as the strong lad joined gang behind tree
The first of the honkers reached bread covered feet

Now ducks at a bread feast aren't known for turn taking
And clumsy are webbed feet when not on pond skating
And when the first fast one stopped quickly in time
A big bunch of back ones barged in from behind

Now honkers in first place of race had been fast pushed
Through small gap in tent flap by back end of duck rush
And as the back end lads grabbed foot parts with beaks
The tent filled with wing flaps and girly type shrieks

Now whilst we were well-hid and watching tent madness
The beard one had stepped out from shower block behind us
And standing there peeking round thick side of tree
With bread bag in strong hand was not place to be

He watched from behind us the tall lad quick fly out
Of small tent in Y-fronts with leg pecked by duck snout
And saw that a small host of ducks were fast following
And honking like old trains whilst fast bread edge swallowing

The beard one then grabbed hold of left ear of strong lad
And led him to small tent with arm swinging bread bag
And badged one who'd earned badge for lots of crime solving
Had quick worked out duck feast had us deep involved in

Now this was like bad time when poor auntie's kitchen
Had small hole in high roof with bath water dripping
And standing on landing in short kind of line
Were me and two cousins awaiting the eye

Stood there we had with just certain parts damper
Than swimsuit type outfit in wrestlers wash hamper
And listening we'd heard them quick climbing up stairs
The footsteps that came with the eyeball of stares

And so it did happen, that eye slowly watched us
As questions were fast asked in way that would catch us
And make us say something to prove that we'd been in
The room above kitchen where raining was ceiling

Now things would have gone well if aunt hadn't noticed
That filled bath with plug in had Action Man floating
And footprints that led from the bathroom had toes
And something not left by a tap-turning ghost

So stood there we were with the whole campsite woken
By screaming of girl voice and wing-flap commotion
And every tent in there had head stuck out staring
At long lad in Y-fronts and nothing else wearing

You could say that campers were strange in their own right
By choosing to tent up and freeze on a wet night
But normal they now looked in light of duck drama
And wandered round big field in red striped pyjamas

I don't need to tell you that gang was bad treated
And made to wash pots up for whole crowd of eaters
And last in the food line at back of the queue
Had left us with burnt bits and bits that were chewed

Now someone from scout group had heard it was said
That badged one had new scar and bandage on leg
And this had confused us for lad had got wound
From hero type actions on day trip to zoo

We'd heard that whilst walking past tiger type housing
He'd heard voice of small child who'd fallen in shouting
And when he'd quick jumped in to rescue the child
He'd got a good mauling from something quite wild

A good thing for him was that tiger got tooth caught
In white sock while long arms and four paws of claws fought
But long lad was stronger and climbed back to top
With small child in one arm and tiger on sock

We heard that the zoo had to close while they caught it
And long lad was well fussed and free pass rewarded
And badges he'd have soon for high zoo cage climbing
And carrying of children whilst tiger type fighting!!

The Green Head of Man

Now parents would always be told off by granddads
For spoiling the fun of the mud covered gang lads
And once I had seen mine get dad in a headlock
And rub top of dad's head with knuckle on bald spot

The granddad that I had was big bald and sockless
And chased us round small house like nimble foot boxer
And told us of big fights with rats and Jack Russells
And men that built railways with just spades and muscles

So visiting parents of parents were good times
And on this day early we drove off to seaside
To meet with the old ones with cakes of all colours
The big parent scarers and ornament lovers

The kitchen of grandnan was small and was filled with
A whole host of family avoiding the dog dish
And as we danced round it like handbag at wedding
The dog watched us keenly in case we dipped bread in

Now this dog was barking and twice wide as long
As lumpy as gravy with teeth mostly gone
Worn down by chomping and chewing of stones
And anything else that was kicked, tossed or thrown

Now this day we'd found poor old grandnan in sad mood
For chicken that lived in the garden had been chewed
And strange thing about it was no marks were found
From teeth on the limp thing there chewed on the ground

Stories like these are remembered by families
Like big one when spaniel got ear caught in mangle
And one such big story I heard there that day
Was one about big fish that quick slipped away

Now granddad had told me that when he was kid
He'd fished with a bent pin on long piece of string
And a fish called the 'big un' would nip worm off hook
And chomp it in deep place too deep for a foot

And one of his friends who was skilled in fish wrestling
Had jumped in and quick grabbed the 'big un's' back end thing
But battle soon ended when fish did a swimmer
And bloke pulled a hand out to find he'd lost finger

Now granddad had said that the 'big un' still lived there
In pond where he'd washed head when young and had lost hair
And someone had told him that finger still wriggled
In nest made of hair in the 'big un's' fat middle

Now gang wasn't frightened of fish that had chewed on
The finger of man who had new one now glued on
And as we were climbing to tree den we thought
That 'big un' by small hands of gang would be caught

The tree den you could say was not a top notch one
With four walls, a ladder and rain-stopping roof on
No this was an old door with plank on one end
With hook to hang cap-gun for gang den defence

The plans for the tree den had pictures of good bits
Like spy holes and trip wires and rooms that were secret
And even had big net to drop down if needed
On gang from the new street where lawns were well weeded

For this gang was bad gang with pirate flag flying
From roof of a new den they'd built in a high one
And gang could not get close to quick creep inside it
For a four paw with loud jaw was tied up beside it

So there we were planning on high tree branch door plank
When shouting was heard from the voices of new gang
And who would have thought then that all types of madness
Had just knocked on tree door and popped in to join us

For this day the new gang then fooled gang to thinking
That masked man had chased them with spaceship type gun thing
And this we'd believed as from tree den we'd seen
The punch up they'd had with a masked head of green

When green head had charged off to spaceship or something
The new gang had showed us the note it had left them
The note that said thickly in felt tip type black
'Beware of the phantom for I will be back'

We stayed there for long time on tree den planked high door
For easy type target was gang stood on low floor
And whilst tall lad looked out we figured out a plan
To tackle tall space thing with green head of man

But teatime had crept up on lads hid in high leaves
And tums were loud growling for teatime mum grub feed
And as we walked short street to farm gate with spring thing
We noticed that small boys in small gangs were pointing

Now this kept on happening each time someone passed us
And laughs we could hear slip through cupped mouths behind us
And catching a small one not well hid by gate
We learned we'd been fooled and that green head was fake

The new gang had cooked up a plan and had baked it
And we had took big bite and liked what we'd tasted
So faces were red now like monkeys bent over
And joyless we waited for food shout on sofa

The fingers of some kind of fish we were fed with
On plate filled with chips, beans and thick buttered bread which
On my plate was heart shaped with no crust like edges
And name spelt out nicely in windy type veggies

Now after the rib prods and pointing had moved on
And plates were removed by a hand with pink glove on
We sat there in kennel that four paws avoided
And whispered like warriors in big horse of Troy did

We then went to garage and got out the bike
Of parent with basket and bell and lost light
And went into kitchen and found paper bag
Some crayons, a bed sheet and long coat of dads

With crayons we drew eyes on bag and a nose
With bone going through it and mouth partly closed
With just a fang peeping red tipped over lip
And ear which was Spock shaped or Mexican crisp

The sheet we then draped over bike to try hide it
And made it quite horse-like except for the basket
And coat was then held up for me to quick climb in
Whilst small lad was sent off with job of gang finding

The small lad was soon back and told us he'd seen them
In big group stood standing by big house with ghost in
So gang sent the tall lad to spy over hedge
And do secret birdcall if crowd turned its head

We got to the top of the street with no bird sounds
And peeked through a small hole in hedge at the big crowd
And sitting on bike seat I readied for push
From strong lad who'd send horse type bike out in rush

So there I sat waiting on basket-belled stallion
With biggest coat ever and head set for bag on
And when bag was placed and bike pushed with a shout
I learnt then that plan had a few bits missed out

The first was that eyes drawn with crayons might look good
But holes we'd forgotten for real eyes to look through
And then there was big sheet that dangled on ground
Which hid peddle nicely from foot pushing down

So as I flew out onto wide hedge edged pavement
I tried to steer bike straight and not just where wheel went
For straight wheel would keep me from kerb with high edge
So I turned it back straight and went straight into hedge

Now Spock ears weren't needed to pick up the loud sound
Of twenty odd lads who had quickly turned heads round
And as I quick scrambled from hedge with deep gully
I'd guessed that the odd one had found it quite funny

So pulling the bike out I charged towards bird sounds
From gang that was still hid in place I'd have not found
And got round the corner quick whipping off bag
And charged back to dog den to work out a plan

You could say that gang pride had had a slight bashing
When blind horse bike rider went fast high hedge smashing
And something was needed to get back our pride
A lovely big lip smacking tongue-flapping lie

So up street we slow walked and met the crowd waiting
With some still loud howling and crash imitating
And stood there before them with no sign of knowing
How hedge had a bike hole instead of bits growing

We quick claimed that maybe a strange horse had run from
The circus where we'd seen some horsemen with bags on
And parents had warned us that one had got loose
A big one with basket and wheels swapped for shoes

Now some of the lads in the big crowd there waiting
Did not quite believe we were just back from skating
And one thing, a small thing right then was quick noted
That I was stood standing still parent coat coated

Tutting we stood there with eyebrows high raising
While strong lad explained we wore big coats for skating
And just when we thought we'd got pride back quite smartly
Along came a mad voice that burnt down the party

Now a parent that's just found that bed sheet has slug thing
Quick wriggling past footprint on edge bit with hole in
Is not in the best mood for cringing lads shuffling
With fingers on lips sending signals for shushing

No this one was barking and shouting and waving
The bed sheet like start man in fast car type racing
And us with our heads down slow trundled down lane
For long talk on house things that weren't there for play

Other tales will tell of the battles with 'big un'
And park guard that guarded the pond that he lived in
For gang up in high leaves had thought up a plan
A good one with fake snake and wooden hand of man

Foot in Pond

The sunlight fell soft on the tree-scattered garden
Where the dog under bird table lay
The house was a low house with pottery and parents
A bungalow base for the parently aged

Now deep in that garden a secret I had found
In the pond with the willow tree hood
Home to the frogspawn and great crested pop can
And on this occasion, my foot

Now this would be fine if on foot at the time
A high welly boot had been placed
But sockless and bootless I stooped in the gloopness
Of tadpoleness deep as my waist

The day was a Saturday and it's known on a Saturday
That when teachers returned to their graves
Parents replaced them with lessons that taught us
That cleaning and shopping and haircuts are thought as
Much more exiting than things that we thought up
So parents today must be somehow avoided

My plan to escape wasn't nice but I used it
And teased dog with dad's shoe until she had chewed it
And then placed the chewed shoe in middle of the floor
And whilst dad was shouting I slipped out the door

Now outside the backdoor the gang was there waiting
All geared up to tackle the plans we'd been making
In football at school where the best plans were made
Whilst whistle of teacher blew bubbles in rain

Plotting such secrets in PE at school, wasn't easy for I'd forgotten my shorts
And the pair I was issued from lucky dip lost property
Certainly didn't fit me or fashion me properly
And all I could think of while kicking old football
Was how I could keep myself in 'em
For shorts of such hugeness, such tie cordless sky blueness
Had plans of their own and would live 'em

But never the less the plans had been planned
And the deal had been sealed with the usual demand
That on wrist a Chinese burn would be put
If promise was forgotten, not gotten or kaput

The plan was the capture of creature from pond
The promise, to deliver such creature unharmed
Our payment, the full set of Stoke City stickers
For sticker book lacking in red striped-shirted kickers

Now the creature was a newt, a lizard-like frog
That slipped, squirmed and wriggled through tadpoles in pond
And lad had a big pond with no newt to suit
For newts had avoided his newt-hunt pursuits
So approached us he did when our story got round
Of newt in pond slimy the colour of brown

So the deal had been sealed in a goalmouth as soaked
As the shorts I was sporting that were held up by hopes
And I knew that I shouldn't have reached out to shake
For the moving of hand meant the losing from waist
That which was covering as well as my pride
My old Batman Y-fronts and ink stain on thigh

The newt we'd deliver complete and still breathing
With all legs attached and no strings fixed to twitch them
And newt would then walk, slip or slide into home
With windmill in centre and red fishing gnome

We'd needed a plan though so whilst teacher taught
The gang drew contraptions with pieces of chalk
On desk lids and chair tops and backs of our books
Whilst teacher she smiled at our note-taking looks

The problem we had was that newt was stuck fast in
Once submarine of pond war and also red pop tin
And sharp is the entrance of wartime sub sunken
And a place that we couldn't fit a finger to poke him

We knew that we wouldn't get much help from the Navy
But lucky for us we had planned a good plan B
We'd bait newt with newt food 'til from can was free
Then take newt as newt ate to jam-jar with leaf

We thought we would catch it like fish with a hook
And not by a finger for it could be mistook
For some kind of food for a newt to stick tooth in
Or claw that was hidden in a rubbery-type foot thing

Now someone had said once that long things with legs
Like long things to live in and stick out their heads
To grab food with long tongue of slipper-like shape
That's sticky like long slug, not slippery like snake
So all that we needed to find was some bait
Of incredibly cunningly newt food-like shape

Not one of us knew what was food to a newt
And cleverly we guessed it would not be a fruit
And probably not birds, dogs, cats, sheep or mice
Probably something not very nice
So we decided on turnip, fresh from the heap
And carved it to look like a fly

It may have been bigger than nature had planned
And a fly in all truth did not look like a hand
But we figured a pond newt might not know all types
And a green orange hand thing would probably be liked

So onto one finger or should I say wing
We fastened a shoelace for shortage of string
And buzzing we hovered it over the surface
So lifelike was fly-like green orange hand turnip

Now five minutes later we knew we'd been scuppered
By slyness of brown newt not hungry for supper
So fly we let fly over tall garden wall
And a new plan was planned and the best plan of all

We thought if we caught the sly newt in a boot
We could plug it with sock to stop newt getting loose
So first thing we needed was foot to lose boot
For a foot in a boot left no place for a newt

So we drew sticks to choose quick whose leg would lose boot
And as usual with head down I drew shortest shoot
I'd no luck with guessing games, girl talk or raffles
At Christmas would always get small end of cracker
So proudly I stood there like hopscotch game lover
With bare foot on one side and boot on the other

The boot was then hidden beneath Action Man clothing
The safest place ever for a newt to quick jump in
A tangle of hats, coats and jungle-type outfits
Some damaged by battles with holes from shot out bits

So pop can was placed there in front of the boot
And can was then scratched with a willow tree root
We hoped that the scratching would scare newt to boot
And boot could be socked before newt could get loose

We learnt then a lesson while tree root was scratching
That nothing was certain in world of newt catching
For as we were waiting a whirlwind of paws
Arrived with tongue flapping from left side of jaw

The dog grabbed the can and then charged like a mad 'un
To other side of pond as we tried hard to grab him
But dog was built better for speed than the gang
And the jumping and bouncing quick shook up the can

Now the shaking of can emptied can of the beast
The beast from the can which then flew right at me
Who stood there more bird-like, flapping my wings
Than newt was that flew fast towards me from tin

And stepping back swiftly with face stretched as long
As the build up to a sneeze my foot went in pond
And what was amazing and almost guaranteed
Was that bare foot it was that now squelched in the weed

The newt came to land then on leg that was high up
Which stiffened as stiff as the spare leg of pirate
And you'd never believe such a thing could be true
But the newt it did grin as it jumped back in pool

Now lessons are learnt well on days such as these
During newty adventures in ponds under trees
But sometimes when young some mistakes are forgotten
For it wasn't the last time my foot touched the bottom
But what other tales could I tell you today?
If we'd grown up to quickly and made no mistakes!

Sandwich in Sock

The gang was excited like Robinson Crusoe
When one day out walking found shape of a big toe
And sat there in maths class quick counting on thumbs
With thoughts of the playground and battles to come

The battles I speak of aren't types with swords chopping
Or punch-ups in shoe shops when out with mum shopping
No this one was big one when gang of 2d
Would belt filthy conker of gangly 2b

We entered the playground with faces as tough as
A whole bunch of wrestlers along with their mothers
And made way to corner where arms were quick swinging
And those with a full one on string were stood grinning

The 2b boy battlers were stood there and gloating
With conker that some said could never be broken
And others had told us that belter had smashed
Four hundred conkers and didn't have a scratch

So gang walked up slowly with best cowboy faces
And looked in the eyes of the gang that now faced us
The ones that we knew had put slug in the sandwich
Of strong lad who ate half before he had found it

So careful we were to keep eye on these jokers
And checked food for wrigglers and slimy slug pokers
And they did the same for a school play had taught them
That hats should be checked first for glue when they wore them

The rules were loud shouted as gangs were stood listening
By small lad whose small clothes were too big to fit him
The one who in sack race got more than a prize
When he'd jumped out of sack and left trousers inside

When bits on the floor showed which conker was winner
The gang that had lost would then hand over dinner
So hardest brown knobbler was picked from the bunch
So gang wouldn't find that they'd no lunch to munch

So lunch boxes, bags and all pockets were emptied
Along with our shirt sleeves and cases of pencils
And rubbers that smelt nice with bright fruity shapes
Were taken and nibbled as well just in case

Now strong lad of gang had hid sandwich in white sock
But someone had seen him and made him take sock off
And sock was then thrown up on high sports hall roof
Whilst sandwich was put back with rest of the food

At last we were ready and class 2b watched us
As conker was brought out the size of a school bus
And carefully we slipped it on lace that we'd borrowed
From new shoe of parent we'd put back tomorrow

As always it happened and just before first hit
The conker was sniffed to check gang hadn't baked it
And then it was tested for anything at all
That made the brown belter a harder type ball

Now no-one had coin to decide who would bash first
So small lad with eyes shut and finger stuck outwards
Was spun until dizzy then wobbling let loose
And nearest to finger got first choice to choose

Now the lad wobbled more than a Rolf Harris noise
And finger whilst passing poked eye of a boy
Who quick whipped a hand up forgetting one thing
That in it a conker was tied to a string

The conker flew high up as lad covered eye up
And all pairs of eyes watched the conker nut fly
And then there was silence and crowd held its breath
When conker came quick down on dinner ladies head

Now dinner ladies only seemed happy on Fridays
When last dinners over and everything's tidy
And this was the boss one who wore the blue hat
Which now had a place on the top that was flat

Now this dinner lady had eyes that could clear see
From other side of room that a lad had dropped small pea
So I guess that when looking she found it quite strange
That each head in big crowd now faced other way

It seemed like for hours we stared at that wall
At the cricket stumps on low bit that someone had drawn
And some of us whistled, for it's known around school
That when someone's whistling they've not broke the rules

But loud above whistling we heard a new sound
Like flippers of a seal being flapped on the ground
And hands holding conkers now squeezed the nut tight
Each knowing that for conker the time was goodbye

For teacher had come who had high voice with sharp bits
The teacher whose teacup said 'Best Teacher' on it
The one who would struggle hard to slip just one foot in
A four-seater clown car with only three clowns in

Now this was the one who had caught us in kitchen
On sports day when eggs and a spoon had gone missing
And while he'd held egg box in front of our faces
He'd eyeballed us closely for small egg-shaped places

Sports days were good days when parents would teach us
Just how to behave well in front of our teachers
And always we learnt this when dads race began
When dads showed to lads how to act like a man

The dads stood in race line were all kinds of shapes
Big ones and little ones with two things the same
They all wore their trainers and said very loud
That winning's not important it's competing that counts!

So the dads were bent forward awaiting the gun
When one dad quick bolted up track with a run
But in passing was belted by handbag of wife
Then sent back with head down to join the dad line

At last the race started and off dads went charging
Whilst pushing and shoving and grunting and barging
And when one long leg caught on spectator's ankle
Three dads went down in a parent pile tangle

The leader looked back and was laughing so loud
That he didn't see the egg that was thrown from the crowd
Which wouldn't have been too bad and just caused a bruise
If egg at the time wasn't glued to a spoon

A good thing for us was that teacher saw egg sling
And saw that it wasn't hand of gang that had spooned him
So gang was left watching as dads limped and grumbled
And mums cornered race ref for loud four mum rumble

The winner of dads race then ran in slow motion
Past big crowd of bruised dads and egg thrown commotion
And when he raised trophy with a big winning shout
We learnt how competing and not winning counts

Now back in the playground the group had been lined up
Whilst flat foot and blue hat were making their mind up
And crowd was slow wriggling and pulling strange faces
As conkers were hidden in the strangest of places

Now things would have worsened if belters weren't hidden
In underpants and armpits and shirts with tight tuck in
For teacher took loose ones to safe in the staff room
And sent crowd to wait for him quietly in classroom

Now someone had said that when someone was passing
They'd heard from the staff room a strange kind of bashing
And just before break end when lesson bell rang
He thought he'd heard tangling and someone shout "Twangs!"

And as they'd left staff room he'd seen teacher chuckle
At maths one who soft rubbed a bruise on his knuckle
And one had a snake shape on next to thumb finger
And face like he'd seen on a sports day dad winner!

Apple on Foot

One of the lads had thought up a plan
To catch out the noise hating history man
A man made of rules with a skeleton-like shape
With grey hair and glasses and batman-like cape

He dressed like a vampire and the older boys said
That he didn't eat and only drunk drinks that were red
And on hearing these rumours we thought we'd best check
Before fang marks were found after lesson on neck

So spoon from the canteen we took to his room
To see if reflection he had in the spoon
But I think with his power our thoughts he had read
For he took spoon and banged spoon on top of my head

So to catch him we thought we'd ask questions on bats
But were stuck on just how to ask bat stuff in class
So we sat there in silence 'til one brain had plan
Then clever brain told plan to four other brains of gang

Now it happened today that he spoke about kings
About battles and castles and other old things
So we waited and waited and timed well our plan
To pop in the question to pop out a fang

At last the time came and we watched him with eye
As he asked us which king chopped the heads off his wives
And strong lad in gang said as stiffly we sat
"That sir I think was Alexandra the bat"

This I think shook him for speechless he stared
Through dark eyes at strong lad with hand still in air
And as we sat waiting for bat wings to flap
He scratched head and held breath and gave desk a tap

We then noticed teacher was standing in window
With thick blinds behind him the sun couldn't get through
And somehow we needed to lure him to light
To smoke him before he took flight or took bite

The trouble we had was that sun didn't shine on
The table we sat on that he had his eye on
And one table only was one we could use
The one with the girls on with shin-kicking shoes

So somehow we had to swap table with girls
But these girls were mean girls who hid behind curls
And most days the gang was found scratched and well bitten
By the tigers of play time and teacher's cute kittens

So one of the gang thought up plan and quick wrote it
On back of his hand with a felt tip and showed it
To each of us slyly by stretching out yawning
And making a yawn noise that's normal for morning

We needed an apple, some paper and a pin
A piece of chewed paper and something girl pink
And whilst teacher taught about barking old kings
We rooted in pockets and bags for the things

The only thing pink was a prawn cocktail crisp bag
So crisps were quick emptied in mouth of the strong lad
And then we sneaked pin out of corkboard on wall
And chewed up some schoolbook to form a nice ball

We polished the apple on trousers to shine it
And on skin drew love heart with my name inside it
And then we took crisp bag and tied it in bow
And pinned the pink packet to the apple with a note

We thought if the scratchers were told off by teacher
He'd move us to table with sun as a feature
And then we could tempt him from place that was darker
And watch him go off like a teacher-sized sparkler

Whilst eying the scratcher I'd chose as my target
I thought about break time and shin kicks and sharp bits
But that didn't stop me for plan must go on
And this plan would work and would never go wrong!

So I flicked the chewed paper and saw it would reach her
As one of the gang rolled the apple at the teacher
And as the girl pointed with a finger and look
The pink bow tied apple bumped teacher's flat foot

He turned like a parent who'd heard smash in kitchen
To see the girl pointing and me looking busy
And as he picked apple off the floor with a shout
His back clicked and more than a shout came from mouth

We froze when we saw them, the pearly white choppers
Glistening and gleaming like brand new jaw toppers
And as we watched proudly the deeds we had done
We noticed the biters weren't joined to his gums

Quickly he bit down to catch the loose munchers
But flipped them towards us who guarded our lunches
And when they bounced loudly from desk to the floor
They laid there in pieces and ate never more

The teacher now stood there with bad back bent double
Like some kind of scientist with microscope trouble
And on top of the grey head we noticed a bald bit
And fought back the urges we had to use felt tip

And then it was over the lesson was done
With teacher all bended with head to the front
And girls looking grimly and sharpening nails
As gang scarpered quicker than rockets on rails

Something quite strange though I noticed that day
When break time bell rang and we ran out to play
Whilst leaving I'd scooped up the apple from the floor
And on it were teeth marks that weren't there before!!!